The Days After Christmas

The Days After Christmas

John Nieman

To order additional copies of this book, contact:
Xlibris
1-888-795-4274
www.Xlibris.com
Orders@Xlibris.com
770126

Contents

For Janice and Ally

CHAPTER 1

December 24

FOR SEVERAL YEARS now, Lindsay Brinkley actually preferred Christmas Eve to Christmas Day.

A big part of it was the fact that there was still a tiny modicum of anticipation before Santa supposedly came down the chimney after midnight to deposit gifts while his reindeer waited on the roof. Of course, at age sixty-three, Lindsay largely interpreted the fable with a grain of salt. However, partly out of habit and superstition, she really never deposited the gifts under the tree until Christmas morning.

It was a holdover from when her three kids were home. When they were little munchkins, she and her husband would tuck them in bed on Christmas Eve and invite them to dream about a wonderful white Christmas.

Just to get them in the mood, she would play Christmas carols on the stereo for hours. At the time, it would be mostly Bing Crosby, Frank Sinatra, Rosemary Clooney, Judy Garland, Burl Ives, and Nat King Cole.

Over the last decade, she had added a few holiday songs, but those classics were still her favorites. Tonight, she listened to "It's the Most Wonderful Time of the Year."

"Right! Sure! Whatever you say," she mumbled to herself sarcastically.

To try to break this downer attitude, she flipped the music to "We Need a Little Christmas" by Johnny Mathis. She particularly sympathized with the lyric:

> *For I've grown a little leaner*
> *Grown a little colder*
> *Grown a little sadder*
> *Grown a little older*
> *And I need a little angel sitting on my shoulder*
> *We need a little Christmas now*

Instinctively, she knew the sentiment was true and very germane to her current funk. As a concession to the lyric, she did haul out the holly, or at least rearrange it by a few inches on the mantle. Then she put the finishing touches on her Christmas tree. It wasn't much. She felt there were a few too many red ornaments on a few boughs. So she simply rearranged them up or down. Looking at the tree that had been in the same corner of the living room for thirty-two years, she felt it at least represented the spirit of the night before Christmas.

Satisfied that she had done some things to accommodate the season, she then showered to try to wash away any remaining sad thoughts. Ever since she was a young woman, she always found this exercise a reviving experience. She then applied a minimum of makeup and put on a bright-red dress that telegraphed Christmas.

She still had fifteen minutes before she would attend the same December 24 party she had attended for decades. It had become a Christmas custom at the Dimlings, who lived just two doors down the street. Every Christmas Eve, they threw a rather elaborate bash for the neighborhood, complete with catered food and a hired piano player.

When Lindsay's children were young and approximately the same age as the Dimlings, it was great fun to see all the kids giggle about the season and dream of sugarplums. The Dimlings' kids still lived in Westchester County and made a point of attending every year, along with their grandkids. So in some respects, it still had some of the magic of "once upon a time."

Other families that had just moved to the neighborhood also attended with their kids, so the tradition still lived, albeit without Lindsay's offspring.

A few years back, Lindsay actually spoke with Diane Dimling about taking a pass on the holiday party. Mrs. Dimling wouldn't hear of it. "You are a major part of this community and the Christmas Eve party. It just wouldn't be the same without you."

Consequently, she did promise to attend and actually looked forward to the event. It always seemed to be a good and uplifting evening with Swedish meatballs, fresh sliced turkey, and fudge brownies. Little kids always seemed to be running around, up and down the staircases. Wineglasses clinked. Christmas carols were sung by the piano man.

Even on this umpteenth time, it felt good and helped dim the dark outlook that Lindsay had for tomorrow. As she blew kisses to all the new neighbors and hugged some of the Dimling grandkids, she actually sensed a little pep in her step as she walked out the door and felt the snowflakes, which had just begun to dot the street.

"Wow." She smiled to herself as she walked down the porch steps and began to make her way back to her lonely home. It didn't take long for her smile to dissipate.

As she opened the door to her once-bustling family home, she again looked at the lit tree and admittedly did feel a brief flutter of Christmas cheer. Silently, she walked around the empty home, turned out the lights, and sobbed herself to sleep.

CHAPTER 2

December 25

AS SHE SIPPED her morning coffee, Lindsay looked at the crinkled tissue paper, the unneeded cashmere sweater (her third in the color of plum), the brown leather gloves, the not-unexpected chocolate-covered cashews, and the usual assortment of Christmas cards. Rather than reread them for the fourth or fifth time, she decided to take another sip of her French vanilla blend and walk to the picture window.

It was still snowing. There were few drivers on the street and no pedestrians. As a matter of fact, it looked exactly like an idealized romantic postcard.

Of course, postcards do tend to be better than reality. Otherwise, everything in the stores would be selfies. (And who would buy these but the ones who took the pictures?) Instead, she looked back at the Christmas cards for the fifth or sixth time. Here was one with a snowman giving a welcoming wave to the camera. Here was another with two candy canes suggestively intertwined. And here was another that unveiled one family's amazing, extravagant visit to the Egyptian pyramids. It featured the mom and dad and their three prep school kids in front of a triangular landmark. The headline: "A holiday fantasy for the Burkes."

She refused to reread how happy Charles and Kippy Burke were to have been able to afford this Christmas trip to the Sphinx. Yes, yes, yes. It was the most amazing trip that the Burkes had taken in the past twelve months.

Perhaps next Christmas, they could feature Bora Bora. Or perhaps Iceland? Or perhaps New Zealand? Or wait . . . how about the entire family gathered around a Christmas tree in Dobbs Ferry, New York? No, that would be far too pedestrian for the Burkes.

While watching the snowflakes descend upon her driveway, she couldn't help but imagine that everyone on her street was giddily happy with his or her completed checklist of Santa requests. The little ones had surely received their plush toys and flannel PJs. The middle schoolers undoubtedly squealed with glee when they opened their new computer games and athletic gear. On the older end of the spectrum, the married couples would exchange kisses and compliments when they opened up their negligees, vests, ties, and videos of their favorite Netflix or HBO specials.

As she sipped her coffee, she sighed. It was not exactly chagrin. For decades, she had celebrated Christmas like every other occupant on Judson Avenue. Here, she had raised two girls and one boy—all of whom had wonderful and extravagant presents under the tree each and every year. And there was her husband, Brad, who had always surprised her each Christmas morning with a new jewel— usually earrings, but occasionally a bracelet.

Unfortunately, he passed away eleven years ago, just after her youngest son, Todd had moved out of the family home to his new job in Atlanta, Georgia. Her daughters, Leah and Carolyn, had married a decade ago and relocated to Eugene, Oregon, and London, respectively. At the risk of sounding maudlin, the house was never the same. It was the quintessential empty nest. On this late Christmas afternoon, it felt eerily vacant and quiet.

True, Momma Lindsay had traveled to London and Oregon over the years. She had visited her son in Atlanta twice during that time and had a few other visits from her daughters, sons-in-law, and the grandkids. However, given the distance, the difficulty of schlepping the families to and fro in the busiest season of the year (along with inevitable flight delays) was daunting. They always encouraged Mom to make the trip overseas, down south or out west, but after some years, she too grew weary of the airport crowds during Christmas week, which smacked of swarming masses in Kolkata, India.

More to the point, the woman had become convinced that the entire holiday was "all foreplay and no climax" (not that she would ever repeat that phrase to her children or her grandchildren).

As a matter of fact, it seemed as if the drumroll to Christmas started earlier every single year. Once upon a time, the buildup didn't begin until after Thanksgiving. Then it gained a head start around Halloween. Lately, it seemed to gather momentum after Labor Day.

Of course, the last several weeks before December 25 were always frenetic.

And then twenty-four hours later, it all comes to screeching halt. *Poof!* Over and done . . . almost as if the entire crescendo was all for one note.

As she had done for the past dozen years, she called her daughter in London first by ten in the morning and asked if everyone had had a beautiful Christmas.

"Mom, yes! Yes! Yes! The kids are going crazy with all the great presents they received. They love the board games you sent them. They wondered if those games also came as computer versions, but I told them that it would be more fun to gather around the table, roll the dice, and actually interact with each other."

"That was my hope in sending those gifts," Lindsay admitted.

"And, Mom, I also loved the photo album you sent us. Very thoughtful. Did you like the sweater we sent you?"

"My favorite color—plum."

"Did you go to the Dimlings' Christmas Eve party last night? If so, how was it?"

"It was grand," the mom answered, slightly exaggerating.

"Mom, I really wish you could come over to London one of these Christmas years. If you hate the crowds, come a week early and leave after New Year's Day. We have plenty of room and would love to have you."

"Maybe. It's just such a crazy season."

"Tell me about it. Mom, I'm in the midst of making an early dinner for the family. So I'm going to have to get off the phone in a few minutes. Tomato soup and grilled stilton cheese sandwiches. Sound yummy?"

"Yes, Merry Christmas, dear."

"Merry Christmas, Mom. We all love you."

"And I love you all."

After the conclusion of the call, Lindsay tried on the plum sweater and had to privately admit it was a shade different from the other plum sweaters in her closet. She then made herself some waffles with maple syrup and strawberries, her one annual calorie-rich departure from her daily diet. As she indulged in the delicious treat, she again looked out the window and played the Dean Martin duet of "Baby, It's Cold Outside."

Again, she loved the music and the tease of the song. It reminded her when she used to walk holding hands with her late husband, Brad, from the Christmas Eve party. Such fun times. So many years ago. So sexy. So Christmassy.

> *I really can't stay (but, baby, it's cold outside)*
> *I've got to go away (but, baby, it's cold outside)*
> *The evening has been (been hopin' that you'd drop in)*

So very nice (I'll hold your hand, they're just like ice)
I really can't stay (baby, don't hold out)
Oh, but it's cold outside

It brought back such warm memories as she finished her waffles and looked at the gathering frost on her front windows. It was such a good marriage for so many years and particularly painful at this time of year, when she would see and hear so many couples walking hand in hand, either on TV or in the malls.

She had always imagined they would be together into old age. What she loved most about him was that, in addition to being a wonderful, caring father, he was a spectacular husband. Even with three kids, he always insisted that he and Lindsay would take a private vacation every year–just the two of them. Just for romance.

Rather than dwell on the eternal loss, she decided it was time to call her two other children in the US time zones.

Both were cheerful and thankful for the gifts they had received from their mother and had a busy chitchat as they watched their kids scramble around the house and argue about who had first dibs on their recently opened Christmas toys.

"Come to Atlanta next year," her son urged his mother. "Mom, it's not that far from New York. Just a two-and-half-hour flight."

"Come to Oregon for the holiday and escape the cold weather," her daughter encouraged Mom.

"I'll see. I'm not sure that will work for me during the holidays . . . but the airplanes run in both directions."

"I don't know, Mom. It's almost impossible to travel at that time of year with a young family."

"I know, honey. Merry Christmas to you and the kids."

"And a very, very Merry Christmas to you, Mom."

On the heels of these calls to her children, Lindsay looked again at her presents under the tree and popped one of the chocolate-covered cashews into her mouth.

She thought of watching *Miracle on 34th Street* for the umpteenth time by herself but felt it might be just too maudlin for her mood. Instead, she turned to channel 4 to get a feel for the local news. There were the obligatory scenes of the Rockefeller Center tree, the skaters on the rink, and then a feature story on the people who actually had to work during Christmas Day–police officers, firefighters, and even some restaurant waitresses.

However, the story that got her thinking was a ninety-second segment that showcased the Santa Claus from Macy's, the Santa from Bloomingdale's, the Santa from Bergdorf's (who seemed to be dressed better than the others), and the Santas from all the main malls in the city and Westchester County. After an initial tribute to coming down all the chimneys and patiently listening to hundreds of children's wishes, the segment became surprising personal for Lindsay Brinkley.

As one Santa admitted, "It's a funny season for me. I feel I do such good and then bingo! It's all over. And I have to wait another eleven months to do my job."

Another Santa said, "I don't know what I'll do tomorrow. I guess just walk around the city aimlessly."

Another Santa said, "I wish it weren't such a one-day event. Don't get me wrong, it's a great day, but people sometimes lose that Christmas spirit the day after Christmas."

"I know exactly how you feel," Lindsay talked to the television set.

Someday, Lindsay would like that to change. Perhaps tomorrow. As the woman finished her coffee and watched the nighttime snowflakes, she dreamed that a more even season would indeed be nice, if only for all the Santas, if only for herself.

CHAPTER 3

December 26

AS LINDSAY HAD learned from her English grandmother in the mid-1960s, there was once a custom and, in fact, a name for December 26. The Brits always called it Boxing Day, and still do in this new millennium. In its early years, it existed as the official day when companies gave their employees gifts, clothing, and surprises in boxes. In time, of course, this practice was replaced with Christmas bonuses and office parties–all of which now take place in the weeks before Christmas.

However, the custom of Boxing Day still exists in Great Britain. It remains an official holiday in the UK. (My god, the Brits do know how to keep a heritage alive decades after it has faded in its current usage.)

However, these days, it is primarily a sports holiday and a post-Christmas shopping holiday—all of which somehow contributed to the postholiday malaise and psychological hangover that Lindsay had come to believe had infected US culture.

On the day after Christmas, Lindsay turned on the *Today Show* and heard a barrage of commercials for the "best shopping day of the year!" Imagine, reductions of up to 50 percent for all the items that no gift givers thought were worthy enough to put under the Christmas tree. Wow, here's the chance to buy all the items no one really wanted.

It's also a historically major "returns day." Here's your chance to stand in line for several hours to bring back that extra Bloomingdale's skillet you didn't really need or the blouse that was sized just a little too small.

As she listened to this depressing televised agenda for the day after Christmas, she began feeling sorry for herself. Suddenly, she was reminded of the commercialism of the holiday.

More importantly, she felt there was so little to do in the days ahead. It was the same emotion that the out-of-work Santas expressed on last night's telecast. Inevitably, she identified with that emotion. After all, it's the abrupt end of holiday cheer that bugged her . . . But what if the season could somehow be extended? What if the spirit could endure just a little longer? Yes, but how?

Just to fix herself on this dilemma, she poured herself a day-after eggnog and listened to "The Twelve Days of Christmas," as recorded by Burl Ives:

On the first day of Christmas, my true love gave
to me
A partridge in a pear tree.
On the second day of Christmas,
My true love gave to me two turtle doves
And a partridge in a pear tree.
On the third day of Christmas . . .

Yes, it was an old-fashioned Christmas list, Lindsay admitted. But at least it implied that Christmas should be more than a one-and-done holiday. Most importantly, she believed perhaps it could inspire a more modern list, a more personal list of people that should have an extended Christmas season.

She searched for a tablet by her desk and handwrote the new "Twelve Days of Christmas"–actually the "Twelve Days after Christmas." She couldn't sing, and it didn't rhyme, but it did give her a renewed sense of purpose for the next few weeks.

Obviously, there would be one dramatic difference from the original Burl Ives version. Instead of twelve days of gifts for her, Lindsay's modernized list cataloged what she might give other people–the unsung heroes who perhaps might appreciate Christmas extended beyond December 25.

Number one on the list were the Santa Clauses who inspired the thought in her and were now out of a job for eleven months. Her idea was this: if she could somehow anonymously create a day-after-Christmas stocking for each of them, it might acknowledge and glorify their unique contribution to society, on behalf of all the wee ones that sat on their laps and believed.

To effect this, she went to local Walgreens and bought a dozen Christmas stockings at the day-after 50 percent off rate, as predicted on the *Today Show*. She filled each with candy bars, playing cards, chocolate-covered cherries, and Listerine (for all the kids who hugged and kissed him), and a bright-red tie.

Inside this package, she also handwrote a note to each man.

> Dear Santa,
>
> I am writing this the day after Christmas and simply want to thank you for the generous goodness you share during the holiday season. As I hope you know, you are the most amazing figure of love, compassion, family, and charity. Here's my simple, grateful thank-you for representing all the right values in life. I just want you to know there are people who truly appreciate your influence and believe it lasts longer than one day . . . or one season.
>
> X, an anonymous admirer

Satisfied and buoyed by the note, Lindsay created a dozen drop-off points for this day after Christmas. Atop each stuffed stocking, she simply wrote a Post-it note to please deliver to the man who played Santa Claus here at Macy's. Or Bloomingdale's. Or Bergdorf's. Or Westchester Mall. Or Ridge Hill. Or any of the other half-dozen places that she imagined must have employed a Santa Claus at the lowest minimum wage.

Most of these places have a help desk or security station, where she simply volunteered the package and assumed it would ultimately get to the man who devoted the month to be being Santa Claus. As a cheerful woman with a happy face, few doubted her sincere intentions.

It took her about nine hours to deliver all these packages. At 9:00 p.m., she trudged into the house more inspired than she had ever felt in years about the Christmas seasons.

For the first time in days or even months, she smiled broadly and even giggled at the ingenuity of the act. By God, it felt good to at least acknowledge so many who had done so much good.

She poured herself another eggnog and turned on the stereo. By 10:00 p.m., she was listening again to "The Twelve Days of Christmas." A good list, she believed. But she firmly believed her list was even better, more needed, and more meaningful in today's world. Encouraged by the day, she even mentally scheduled who would be next, and then next. She also began to catalog what kind of surprise presents would be most appropriate for each of her targets. It would take some work. It would take some time. But in her heart, she knew it would be worth it.

At the conclusion of the song, Lindsay felt alive again. For the first time in at least ten years, she went to bed and felt she was not just a bystander in life. Unlike the sobs of the prior two evenings, she actually smiled and fell fatigued but easily to sleep.

CHAPTER 4

December 27

INSPIRED BY HER Good Samaritan act last night, Lindsay woke up without an alarm clock and felt some true holiday spirit before 8:00 a.m. As she walked around her wonderful, albeit outgrown, family home, she felt fortunate.

It had four true bedrooms, which were rarely used these days but still brought such fond memories of her kids' early years when they would jump on the beds, which were usually stacked with plush toys. Normally, this walk down memory lane would depress her. It might even prompt a call to her daughters or son to just say hi and silently flash on the good old days. However, she didn't feel compelled to do so this morning.

As she walked down the stairwell to the main floor, she plugged in the Christmas tree and poured herself a cup of coffee. The room was a grand master kitchen that once upon a time prepared elaborate family dinners and Thanksgiving feasts. Even though it hadn't been used for this purpose for so many years, it still had all the amenities–a double door refrigerator and freezer, an eight-burner Viking oven, a state-of-the art microwave, and plenty of gadgets, which, these days, just gathered dust.

When the home was bustling, Lindsay was actually quite an accomplished cook. As a matter of fact, she often prepared meals for her husband, her kids, and their friends. However, as her life changed, these occasions became more rare. And as an empty nester, she had no interest in putting on an apron to make a meal for herself.

As she took her cup of coffee into the dining room, all these gatherings surfaced in her mind. Just by squinting, she could see the kids sipping their soup and tossing their string beans across the table. Such a great home. Such great years. *I suppose that era is done*, she thought.

Almost out of habit, she hit the carousel on her stereo and heard the 1954 hit from Perry Como called "Home for the Holidays." Here's a refresher:

> *Oh there's no place like home for the holidays*
> *For no matter how far away you roam*
> *If you want to be happy in a million ways*
> *For the holidays, you can't beat home, sweet home*
> *I met a man who lived in Tennessee*

He was headed for Pennsylvania and some homemade pumpkin pie . . .

Ironically, she felt lucky. She actually had a home that had good memories. So many people had less. They lived in boxes on the heating grates of New York or trudged into a shelter just to get a good meal with no cell phone or any connection to any of their relatives. They are souls lost in space—with no one to love and no one to love them. Forget home for the holidays! How about a warm meal for the holidays?

As she looked at her elegant kitchen, she pulled out a large stockpot and some cutting knives and refreshed her memory for her favorite Christmas soup. Of course, she didn't have the ingredients, but it was only a five-minute drive to the local A&P, where she could buy ample butternut squash, onions, and chicken stock.

Before she left, she went online and found five homeless shelters in Westchester County. One by one, she dialed the numbers. "How many homeless people do you have in your facility?"

Answers: "Thirty," "Forty," "Fifty," "One hundred," "One hundred fifty."

"Would it be OK if I made them a Christmas soup and brought it to you?"

Pause. Pause. Pause. "How much per bowl?"

"It's a gift," Lindsay responded and further explained. "A Christmas contribution. No charge. I just want to know if you will accept it at the front desk."

Answers: "Of course," "Wow," "That would be wonderful," "We love people like you," "Merry Christmas."

Doing the tally and the math, she prepared enough soup for four hundred people. Culinary secret: If you can make soup for twenty people, it's not that much more difficult to make it for four hundred. Just twenty times the recipe. Yes, it amounts to a lot more cutting, a lot more deep pots, and a lot more Tupperware containers. But hey, isn't that the purpose of an A&P?

All told, it took about three hours of shopping, slicing, and simmering to make enough soup for four hundred hungry, lonely people. OK, let's not oversimplify; it also took measured plastic containers, MapQuest directions to each of the homeless shelters, and enough soupspoons and soup bowls for all the receivers.

By and large, it was a fairly easy and grateful handoff to all the homeless shelters in arguably the wealthiest county in America. Most of the good souls at the front desk were gleeful.

Lindsay brought in the measured portions to each of the homeless shelters.

At the first four locations, she was greeted as an absolute heroine. However, on the fifth location in Yonkers, New York, the front desk personnel wanted verification that her delivery was authorized.

Lindsay looked at her notes and told the woman at the front desk that a certain Ms. Bostock had encouraged her to bring the butternut squash soup for the one hundred homeless people in the shelter.

"Ms. Bostock left no note at the front desk to clear this delivery," the officious woman said.

"So what are you saying?" Lindsay responded. "Your one hundred homeless people do not wish to have a homemade butternut squash soup?"

"I just don't know that it has been cleared," the front desk bureaucrat responded.

After several calls to her superiors, the tired civil servant sighed and acknowledged the aromatic gift from Lindsay and accepted it without a simple thank-you.

Somewhat disappointed by the "Who are you?" inquisition of the butternut squash soup delivery in Yonkers, Lindsay walked back to her car and reminded herself that is was all worth it. It was worth it discovering that people less fortunate than the Brinkley family could, in fact, have a wholesome meal tonight. It was worth it to thank the lonely Santa Clauses. Most importantly, it was all definitely worth it to rediscover the true spirit of Christmas.

Once she had returned to her home, she warmed up a bowl of the pumpkin soup and quietly enjoyed the flavor. She also couldn't help but imagine that all those homeless people might have a similar smile on their faces as they tasted every spoonful.

CHAPTER 5

December 28

WHEN LINDSAY WOKE up on Sunday, she felt a sense of accomplishment for her good deeds over the past few days. Under her comfy duvet, she enjoyed the warmth of the bed for a good ten minutes. Eventually, she walked to the window to see the weather conditions of the day. At 8:00 a.m., it was just a snow flurry—a rather light and pretty one at that.

To match the mood, she poured herself an early cappuccino and thought of calling her daughter Leah in London to report on her recent transformation. As the mom reminded herself, it would probably come off all wrong—as if she was bragging about being such a good person. Worse yet, it could come off as an admonition to her daughter to be a more giving individual. The one thing Mrs. Brinkley believed she had learned over the past few days was that none of her actions were about notoriety. As she often privately admitted to herself, she was actually getting more out her behavior than what she was giving other people. *It's a weird irony*, she thought. Charity is its own reward.

She took another sip of her cappuccino and hit the Play button on her stereo. Almost on a simpatico cue, she heard Rosemary Clooney begin to sing "Let It Snow."

Though the weather outside is frightful
And the fire is so delightful
But if we've no place to go
Let it snow, let it snow, let it snow
Man, it doesn't show signs of stopping
And I've got me some corn for popping
The lights are turned way down low
Let it snow, let it snow, let it snow

Instinctively, she also turned on the TV. As she skipped around the dial, she finally settled on the *Today Show* and watched Al Roker give a double-warning weather report.

"For starters, it's a beautiful thing right now, and it will be for the next several hours. So if you need to run some errands, do it before four p.m.," Roker warned. To demonstrate, the weatherman held out his hand and caught the snow in his glove and blew the crystals in the air. "However, by six p.m., it will turn into a blizzard. You will *not* want to be on the road.

"Now just to prepare all you long-distance travelers, this is perhaps bad news for anyone who has a flight tonight. And bear in mind, this is one of three biggest travel days of the year. Yes, there is Thanksgiving. Yes, there is the week before Christmas. But tonight–Sunday night–this is when everyone waits till the last minute to get home to Atlanta or Charlotte or Dallas or wherever.

"We anticipate all the flights from JFK, LGA, Newark, and Westchester will be delayed by several hours starting at seven to eight p.m. So if you've got a family, get some potato chips, sandwiches, and soft drinks, because you might have a long wait in the airline terminals."

The Al Roker report was akin to opening up a barely healed, ugly Christmas wound. For three years in a row, she was stranded at the New York airports as she attempted to visit her three children. It took no imagination for her to remember the frustration and the near-total lack of communication for the airline personnel about when the flight might eventually lift off.

And so Ms. Lindsay assumed a new mission of this beautiful snowy Sunday.

While the streets were still quite passable, she went to Barnes and Noble to buy every Christmas record they might have. To her surprise, they had almost four hundred Christmas-oriented CDs that had not sold by now. She bargained to buy them all on one condition: "Could Barnes and Noble please wrap each CD individually?" Yes, of course, they would. After all, money talks, especially with CDs that are destined for storage for the next twelve months. With a credit card in the amount of four hundred dollars, she was able to clear out all the unsold and discounted Christmas CDs, as long as they could be packaged.

While she was at it, she decided to replenish her supply of more recent holiday recordings. Armed with four bags of music, she headed to her car to write a note for all the recipients:

Dear airport/airline elf,

I realize you would probably rather be with your own family on this snowy holiday rather than deal with disgruntled travelers who will most likely be delayed for hours on this very busy travel day. Just bear this in mind: you make their holiday possible. And a smile goes a long way into making their day. Hope this CD can revive your Christmas spirit after a weary day. Thanks for all you do. Ho ho ho.

Then she signed each one "Santa's secret helper."

Lindsay put about fifty CDs in each of the bags and checked the weather. The snow was still coming down but had not yet turned into a blizzard. Even so, she decided that it made more sense to hire a car service to deliver each of these to the four New York airports. After all, if it really started to turn into a legit blizzard, she did not want to get snarled in traffic. Also, a car service could take her to the arrival zones, where she could quickly gift the bags to a curbside check-in gentleman, who could distribute to the airport and airline employees.

Given the inclement weather conditions, she dressed warmly–with a snug stocking cap and a heavy winter coat with a hood that she could pull up if it really started to snow heavily.

Despite the gray skies and dropping temperatures, the highways were still relatively clear, other than the Van Wyck, which always had a habit of becoming jammed at the slightest inclement weather. Undeterred, her knowledgeable driver negotiated side streets and arrived at several terminals at JFK airport. One by one, Lindsay brought the black plastic bags to the curbside check-in personnel and encouraged them to distribute the contents to as many crewmembers, pilots, and baggage handlers as possible.

"Oh, and keep one for yourself," Lindsay told the redcap. "And Merry Christmas." The somewhat surprised baggage handler accepted the bag, ran it through the security checkpoint, and returned to his station.

Meanwhile, Lindsay and the driver headed to the LaGuardia and Newark Airports, where she repeated the same procedure. Her last stop was the Westchester Airport, where she dropped off her last gift bag and climbed back into the black sedan. As she entered the back seat, Lindsay heaved a big sigh of relief that she had actually completed her mission.

"It's getting worse, isn't it?" she asked.

"At this point, it's hour by hour," the driver answered. "I think in about two hours, it's going to be a whiteout nightmare. And where to now?" the man asked.

"Back home," she answered and sank back into the leather seat, quite satisfied that she had the foresight to order a car service rather than risk the drive in her own car.

As she watched the gathering storm, she felt she had done a service for all the stranded travelers and the airport personnel. Yes, the roads were getting more challenging. She was aware of the fact that the driver had reduced his speed by half and was more aware than ever about the cars to his left, right, and behind and was thankful for his safety measures.

Within the next hour, she arrived at her home. Presented with the bill, she left a generous tip to the man behind the wheel and gave him one of her few remaining CDs. "Maybe you can enjoy this tomorrow," she advised. "Thanks for being so careful on the roads."

With that, she exited the car and carefully climbed the pathway to her home. She discovered that there were at least eight inches of snow on each of her porch steps, but holding the railing, she was able to get in the house safely. Instinctively, she waved goodbye to her driver, who was easing out of her driveway.

Ensconced in the warmth of her home, she poured herself a rare Jack Daniel's and saluted herself for such a contribution on this weather-challenged adventure. It reminded her of the late evenings when she and her husband, Brad, would occasionally have a nightcap and recap the day.

Those were good days, she reflected to herself and took a small sip. *And these are good days*, she reminded herself.

CHAPTER 6

December 29

T HE MORNING NEWS was yin-yang of good news and bad news.

Despite flight delays of several hours last night, interviews with the stranded travelers were surprisingly benign. As a matter of fact, many travelers actually complimented the airline personnel for trying their best to accommodate their busted schedules and missed connections. Some complimented the employees for serving complimentary hot cocoa. A few offered kudos for the fact that the airline personnel did their best to keep their spirits high despite weather conditions beyond their control. One woman even praised them for playing Christmas music through the intercom between flight announcements.

"Yes!" Lindsay held up her triumphant fist and couldn't resist a satisfied smile.

"And that brings us to our next story related to the airports," the newscaster continued. "Evidently, a Good Samaritan woman who identified herself as Santa's secret helper brought gifts for all the airline employees yesterday in the middle of the snowstorm. It appears as if she visited all the NY airports. According to one curbside baggage handler, she quickly dropped off wrapped CDs for the airline employees who were weathering the storm."

The redcap smiled and said, "It lifted all our spirits on a very difficult day. She didn't ask for anything in return. She just gave me the bag and asked me to distribute to my fellow employees. And then she was gone! Hey, Santa's helper. Merry Christmas to you!"

When the newscast cut back to the reporter, he too was complimentary. "We don't know who she is or where she lives. Perhaps the North Pole. But given the security cameras at the airports these days, here's a blurry picture of Santa's secret helper." He then let the tape roll on a jerky, rather out-of-focus film of Lindsay in her stocking cap and pulled-up hood bringing a black bag to one of the curbside employees. There was only a fleeting second when the camera caught a profile of her face, and the snowflakes in the foreground made the image even less recognizable, but even so, it upset her. Aghast, Lindsay looked at the quick footage and uttered a rather loud "No!"

The newscaster continued, "We would just simply like to know this woman. So if any of my viewers recognize her, we will try to get in touch with her, celebrate her contributions, and better understand her good motives."

Again, Lindsay exclaimed, "No!" The whole idea that she might be outed was anathema to her. In a perverse way, it would undermine the goodwill and the positive emotions that she had begun to feel every day.

Almost immediately, she turned off the TV and revisited her list of things to do for the twelve days of Christmas. Perhaps she should just call it "mission accomplished" and get on with her lonely life. Looking at the tally, she realized she had barely accomplished half the good deeds she had hoped to fulfill. What would be the downside in calling it quits? Well, for one thing, more than 50 percent of the people she hoped to help would be left in the dark. Just as importantly, she would feel that she had given up. She had already felt that emotion over the past several Christmas seasons. If she gave up now, she believed it might do irreparable damage to the progress she had made over the past five days.

Obviously, it would be increasingly difficult to stay anonymous. In an effort to complete her private mission, she decided she might need a disguise. She headed to her closet and found her favorite big sunglasses–the big ones that covered half her face, Audrey Hepburn style. Combine that with a winter scarf over her chin and she could go almost anywhere incognito. Just to complete the masquerade, she dusted off a fedora from her late husband. If she poofed her hair under the brim, who would ever recognize her?

Satisfied with her new look, she sat in the big leather chair in the living room.

She then walked over to the mirror and admired the attire, particularly the chapeau that inevitably reminded her of her late husband, Brad.

He was a good man, and in all honesty, his passing had created a chasm in her life. In the past six or seven years, her children had encouraged Lindsay to perhaps join Match.com or at least entertain a suggestion from one of her friends to fix her up with a friend of a friend or a recent widower or a hardworking neighbor that someone in an adjoining community somehow knew.

Lindsay always demurred. However, wearing the hat, she did long for those days when she had a man who would listen attentively to her ups and downs, commiserate on her life, share a laugh, and perhaps even give her a hug.

She took off her Audrey Hepburn sunglasses, squinted, and could easily imagine her dear late husband. She then grabbed the stereo remote control and flipped songs until she found the one that perfectly matched her mood. It was the Elvis hit called "Blue Christmas":

> *I'll have a blue Christmas without you*
> *I'll be so blue just thinking about you*
> *Decorations of red*
> *On a green Christmas tree*
> *Won't be the same, dear*
> *If you're not here with me*

And when those blue snowflakes start fallin'
That's when those blue memories start callin'

Lindsay listened to entire song and instinctively put on the sunglasses to mask the tears rolling down her cheeks. Truth be told, she had not cried since Brad's funeral. It's not that she wasn't emotional all these years. She grieved. She missed the unexpected moments. And she steeled herself to get by another day. The woman did have and still possesses an amazing capacity to move forward. She truly felt this progress in the past week, but today was definitely a setback.

In a symbolic expression of enduring love, Lindsay approached the mirror, kissed the glass, and then blew a Christmas kiss to her long-lost husband.

CHAPTER 7

December 30

IN AN EFFORT to revive her spirit, Lindsay revisited her list of twelve things to accomplish after Christmas. She circled all eight remaining missions as important and decided to bridge the gap between what was done and what still needed to be done.

Instinctively, she readjusted the order of things and was relieved that the next few chores would theoretically be quite easy to execute–with or without an elaborate disguise. Given the fact that she lived near the Ridge Hill Shopping Center, she decided to stock up on gifts early in the a.m. before the Westchester crowds invaded this beautiful shopping center.

According to her accounting, she would need approximately two hundred more presents for the forgotten souls that made her world comfortable. In addition, she tallied that she might need at least three hundred more gifts for the sad, the lonely, and the lost souls.

In a reflex reaction, she took out her checkbook and discovered she still had about a thousand dollars in the bank. As she reluctantly admitted to herself, it was not an infinite budget. But it was only a few days until her social security check would be automatically deposited. Besides, most people spend money on stupid things, and as Lindsay reminded herself, her gifts weren't exactly stupid.

In anticipation of the days to come, she visited four different stores within the center and bought a variety of presents, some of which were specifically tailored for an audience or a dedicated group of people. She also bought some items that she could mix or match if the occasion presented itself. It was quite a cache of unique presents.

Carrying four large bags of new gifts, she struggled down the sidewalk and successfully loaded them in the back seat of her jeep. Once she had the packages secured in such a way that the fragile things would not jostle or break, she exited the lot and drove home.

Feeling buoyed and back in the game, she turned on the TV, only to discover that her story was still in the news. "Who is this mystery woman?" the broadcaster asked. "She has certainly contributed to a good holiday season for so many . . . but nobody knows her name. She calls herself Santa's helper, but surely that's not her real name. Call us if you know her."

The camera then flashed her blurry, herky-jerky profile picture. It was evidently from the Newark Airport drop-off. She remembered putting up her hoodie at that stop and foreground snow seemed to match the weather conditions at that time of the day. It was really only a one-second shot with a slo-mo, out-of-focus profile. Given the dark, overcast lighting, even she would have difficulty identifying herself.

Even so, this investigative preoccupation was annoying. Also, it was counter everything she was trying to accomplish during this Christmas gift-giving season.

Frustrated, she immediately switched the dial to another channel. Here, she saw a repeat of a very emotional public service announcement she had seen just yesterday. The main interview was with the director of the Yonkers animal shelter. According to Alice Conrad, "Each year, more than one thousand dogs, cats, and other animals come through our doors. All of them desperately want and need a forever home. Not surprisingly, this is our biggest season. When we can match the right pet with the good family, it's sort of a Christmas miracle."

Her assistant, Janet Ferrara, added, "We have a small staff of eight people, but we depend heavily on volunteers—maybe fifteen this time of year. They all love animals. They hug the dogs, walk them, and nurture them until they can be matched with the right family. You know all volunteering makes you feel good inside, but it's sort of special when the thanks you get comes with a big lick on the face from a four-legged friend."

Lindsay particularly enjoyed the next part of the commercial. It showed a slow-motion lick on the face of a five-year-old boy that giggled like crazy and hugged his new pet.

Then the weird but fun part. It was basically the Christmas classic mixed with dog barks. The effect was as if the shelter dogs were singing the song:

> *Bark, bark, bark*
> *Bark, bark, bark*
> *Jingle all the way*
> *Bark, bark, bark, bark*
> *Bark, bark,,ark*
> *In a one-horse open sleigh*
> *Bark, bark, bark*

Lindsay remembered touching her heart as she watched the end of the PSA. The visual wrapped up with another hug–this one between a big dog and a little girl. And then there were some words and numbers about how to donate a dog or volunteer one's services.

Now that's a damn good cause, Lindsay remembered saying to herself. From personal experience, she appreciated all that a pet can mean to a family. The memory of her own children hugging their beloved golden retriever and fox terrier seemed like yesterday. On her initial list of twelve gift-giving causes, she had vaguely identified animal shelter. On the basis of that particular commercial, she determined that the Yonkers

Animal Shelter should be the recipient of her gift-giving generosity.

Earlier in the day, she had shopped for the ideal gift for pet caregivers. She found just the thing at PetSmart– white ceramic coffee mugs that spelled out the word "love." However, instead of the letter *O*, it featured the stylized paw print. As soon as she saw it, she knew it would be perfect for the pet lovers at Yonkers Animal Shelter.

Fortunately, they had thirty of them, and she bought them all. As she wrapped each of them, she attached an individual note to each present.

> Dear animal-shelter volunteer,
>
> What you do each day is wonderful. To find a loving home for these lonely creatures brings such happiness to so many people. It's truly God's work. And you make it happen. Thank you. Merry Christmas.
>
> X, Santa's secret helper

To be honest, Lindsay felt very little risk of being exposed by these good people. However, just as a precaution, she adorned herself with a costume. She pulled up her hair in a bun. Then she covered it with a dusty cowboy hat from her son's closet. She added wraparound sunglasses and a bright-red scarf. Voilà! She looked nothing like Lindsay Brinkley.

It was 3:00 p.m., the slowest part of the day. Given her newfound caution, it could mean an easier mission. Given the lack of traffic, she parked her car right in front of the shelter and nonchalantly walked through the front door of the institution.

There was a receptionist at the desk just to her left. "Can I help you?" she asked.

"These are for your volunteers," Lindsay stated. "Keep up the good work." As she reached the door, she turned to the receptionist. "And Merry Christmas."

The transaction lasted all of four seconds. As she looked to her right and left, there were no cameras, no danger, no risk of unmasking the mysterious Good Samaritan.

She then walked–almost skipped–to her car, delighted that she had done something good for kindred spirits who were dedicated to doing good every single day. All the way home, she sang "Jingle Bells" and occasionally barked out a line.

What a wonderful season, she thought. *What a wonderful contagious experience it is to deal with so many wonderful people.*

CHAPTER 8

December 31

EVEN AS A college student, Lindsay Brinkley despised the New Year's Eve holiday. She always viewed it as drunken night, and as a barely moderate drinker, she always felt that she was the soberest person at the bar while others simply stumbled and flirted incessantly.

Also, she believed that it truly did prematurely end the Christmas season. True, it was indeed a week after Christmas Eve, but was that any reason to squash the entire season of goodwill and usher in an entire year of debauchery?

Consequently, she refused to celebrate the holiday, partly because she no longer had anyone with whom to celebrate the holiday. Instead, she tried to bridge the gap with a continuation of her Christmas music.

Her choice for the day? One that could somehow connect what was with what might be. It was one of her truly favorite Christmas songs. In this case, she actually turned on her computer to see the video version of the Bing Crosby and David Bowie classic called "Little Drummer Boy."

> *Come they told me*
> *Pa-rum-pum-pum-pum*
> *A newborn king to see*
> *Pa-rum-pum-pum-pum*
> *Peace on earth. Can it be?*
> *Years from now, perhaps we'll see*
> *See the day of glory…*

In the midst of this song, the doorbell rang.

Without turning off the music, Lindsay walked to the door and greeted the stranger. While he looked vaguely familiar, she did not recognize him as someone she knew from the neighborhood. However, she immediately liked his cheerful demeanor.

"My name is Nick Carter," the man said. "And I know who you are."

Somewhat jarred by his last line, Lindsay scanned the yard to see if the man had a posse of strangers ready to rob her home. After looking up and down the street and feeling secure that he was indeed a man alone, she eventually responded, "And who am I?"

"You are Santa's helper," the smiling face responded. "And I am the Santa for a month at Ridge Hill."

"Wow," the woman involuntarily responded. She looked at the man and saw an innocent soul. Atypically, she invited the man into her home.

"Coffee?"

"You got hot cocoa?" the man responded.

"Take a seat," Lindsay responded and put a cocoa cup in her Keurig machine as she rejoined her curious stranger.

Meanwhile, the song on the computer continued to play. "It's one of my favorite Christmas songs," Nick admitted.

"Mine too," Lindsay admitted and asked for a few minutes to pour two cups.

Over sips of the hot cocoa, Nick explained himself. "I am a security guard at Ridge Hill. In December, I double as a Santa Clause in the quadrangle. It's fun, but no one ever says thanks . . . other than you. Who is this nice woman? I asked myself.

"Let me explain. You came into my office with a Christmas stocking. You said 'Give this to Santa Claus.' Guess what, I am the guy who accepts the gift and gives it to Santa Claus, who is me."

"Oh my god!" Lindsay exclaimed, feeling exposed.

"I think I said thanks. Then I follow you with my eyes to your jeep and write down the license number. That, with the recent videos at the airports, leads me to your door this afternoon."

"Damn," Lindsay said, shaking her head in disbelief.

"Whoa, don't worry. Your secret is safe with me. Hey, do you think I want to expose Santa Claus or Santa's secret helper?" Nick eased the tension. "I just want to say thank you . . . and perhaps invite you to a light lunch this afternoon. Obviously, we both have the same charitable drive." He then smiled broadly and chuckled like the real Santa Claus.

Lindsay took another sip of her cocoa and looked at the kind gentleman. Cautious by nature in her interpersonal relations, she smiled and demurred. "I can't do that. At least, not today. I've got good-deed plans for the afternoon. But if you have a card, perhaps I could give you a call when things ease up a little."

Nick reached in his pocket and pulled out his business card from Ridge Hill. His full name was Nick Carter, and his title was security supervisor. "It doesn't list me as Christmas Santa Claus, but that will be our little secret." He chuckled again.

"Well, I just wanted to meet the mystery woman and say hi," he said and moved to the front door. She followed. He leaned over and gave her a hug and a peck on the cheek. "Keep up the good work. And give me a call sometime if you ever want another cocoa." He then left the house and walked to his car.

At the front door, Lindsay followed him with her eyes and waved goodbye. *A little bit of a weird visit*, she thought. *Weird, but nice.* And besides, he was a nice man with good looks. About her age too. Maybe she would someday take him up on his offer for another cocoa.

Food for thought, she told herself. As a matter of fact, the visit set her back for a half hour as she reflected on her otherwise lonely mission. In the process, she realized she had a kindred spirit who quite possibly understood her motivations. However, for the time being, she needed to head to the kitchen and whip up some chocolate chip cookies. She had read that there would be a New Year's gathering for senior citizens at the local embassy center. From some prior volunteer work, she knew that the age span of seniors who would attend such a brunch would be primarily in their seventies and eighties. Some might even be in the nineties. Many would be in wheelchairs or moving slowly. Most would be living alone and would look forward to this event as a time when they could connect with people of their own age frame.

Lindsay couldn't help but think that as the calendar neared the passage of a bright new year, it might be depressing to many of the octogenarians and beyond who might believe their best days were behind them. Consequently, she believed that a delicious taste of childhood might add some sunshine on a cold winter's day.

When she took a bite of a warm cookie from the oven, Lindsay had to admit it automatically made her feel younger.

She anticipated that there would be about one hundred senior citizens at the event, which would normally begin with card games or bingo and culminate with an easy-to-digest meal such as soup, pasta, or meatloaf. They would probably have Jell-O or custard for dessert. But Lindsay had a real hunch that her homemade cookies would be the hit of the party.

She wrapped up four big trays of the warm cookies and added a note to each package:

Dear senior friends in the community,

I want you to know what an amazing contribution you continue to make to the town and simply wanted to wish you a very happy holiday. Enjoy the homemade cookies and your many friends. Merry, merry.

She signed each note "Santa's secret helper."

Then she donned her disguise, including an oversize coat, and headed to the embassy center. Rather than risk being identified again, she waited in the car until she could see a few total strangers, usually accompanied by a younger escort on the outside of the venue. One by one, she would bring a big tray and ask the strangers to bring them inside to the food table.

In about five minutes, she had given away all the cookies and was able to get back in her car for the short ride home. She was confident that no one recognized her and smiled all the way home. When she opened her front door and looked at her costume, she took a quick twirl and indeed felt like a kid again, especially after she took a bite of one of her few remaining chocolate chip cookies.

That night, as she had done on most New Year's Eves, she watched the early fireworks in Australia and Europe but didn't stay up to watch the televised countdown in Times Square. Instead, she snuggled under the comforter and reflected on her full day. Inevitably, she did wonder what Mr. Nick was up to on this New Year's Eve night.

CHAPTER 9

January 1

NEW YEAR'S DAY always struck Lindsay as one of the slowest days of the year. For one thing, the page has turned for so many. The calendars for the year are trashed, and new ones are tacked on the walls. The symbols of Christmas are largely gone. However, for the first time in a decade, Lindsay still had the Yuletide spirit and didn't really want it to end.

The other thing that makes this particular day discombobulating is that nothing is open. All the grocery stories, department stores, and most of the restaurants close. So many people are home, presumably watching nonstop football programming.

Lindsay reminded herself that it's not a free holiday for everyone. The firefighters are giving up a day with their families to stand on call at the firehouse. Also, the police officers are busy at work, making sure the villages are crime-free and that traffic keeps moving. And of course, there are the taxicab drivers, who undoubtedly did yeoman's duty last night and every day, making sure the late-night party people got home safely rather than get behind the wheel.

To reinforce her Christmas mood, she put on one of her favorite Frank Sinatra's hits:

> *Have yourself a merry little Christmas*
> *Let your heart be light*
> *From now on, all our troubles will be out of sight*
> *Have yourself a merry little Christmas*
> *Make the Yuletide gay*
> *From now on, your troubles will be far away*

As she listened to the lyrics, she wrapped gloves for the police officers and firemen. For the taxi drivers in town, she wrapped boxes of chocolates that she still had in her reservoir of gifts.

In her fedora, dark sunglasses, Christmas scarf, and heavy coat, she first drove to the firehouse. Here, she deposited individually wrapped packages of winter gloves with the following note:

Dear Firefighters,

Thanks for keeping our homes safe all year. Stay warm and comfortable this Christmas season.

X, Santa's secret helper.

She simply deposited the big black bag of gifts to the nearest fireman in the house. She then said, "Share with your coworkers, and merry Christmas." With that, she vanished without even waiting for a response.

She had a hunch that ducking into the police department and getting away incognito would be more challenging. Consequently, she decided not to go into the police department. Instead, she looked for a police car on the street. Typical of the stereotype, there was one she found in front of the Dunkin' Donuts. Peering into the window, she could see there were two officers inside sharing a cup of coffee and few glazed cake donuts. Given her penchant for security, she decided it would be best to not enter the shop and risk being identified. Instead, she deposited the next big bag of gifts on the hood of the police car. It contained the following note:

Dear Police Officers,

Please share these Christmas gifts with your fellow officers. Merry, merry.

X, Santa's secret helper

Safely away from the police vehicle, she stayed in her car just to make sure some vandal didn't run away with the gifts. No way. After about ten minutes, the two cops exited the donut store and curiously looked at the bag on top of their car. One looked in the bag and started reading the note to the other guy. They both smiled and looked around the lot to see if the gift giver was there

She was lowered behind the steering wheel about thirty feet away, taking glee in the fact that she had successfully delivered this latest batch of gifts. She stole a look at the two police officers that continued to look to their right and left. After a few moments, they just shrugged, put the bag in the back seat, and drove away.

Without much risk, she figured she could safely deliver the individually wrapped chocolates to the cabdrivers lined up near the train station. There were only four drivers there at this time of the afternoon. She delivered the individually wrapped chocolates with the following note:

Dear Taxi Driver,

Thanks for safely driving people home last night. Merry Christmas and Happy New Year.

X, Santa's secret helper

Casually, she walked up to each of the driver's doors and simply said, "Forgot to give you a tip last night. Merry Christmas." Each driver gratefully accepted the package, and as they began reading the note, Lindsay was off to the next driver with the same message and more delicious Christmas gifts.

By that time, the train had arrived and began filling the taxis with more passengers. Lindsay briskly walked to her parked car and drove out of the lot with another mission accomplished.

It was fun being an anonymous gift giver, she decided. Even on a relatively slow day like today, she had to admit it made Christmas last longer.

CHAPTER 10

January 2

IT WAS NOW more than a week since Lindsay had put up her beautiful Christmas tree. Every night, she would enjoy the twinkling lights, the bright, shiny ornaments, and the star on the top of the tree. She also enjoyed the incomparable aroma of the Douglas fir and did her best to keep it watered every morning. As she bent down with her vase to nourish the growing universal symbol of Christmas, she couldn't help but notice that many of the short green needles had already fallen on the floor. When she brushed across the bottom branches, more needles tumbled.

Unlike past holidays, this made her sadder than she would have imagined. Truth be told, in the last two years, she had dismantled and trashed the tree a few days after

Christmas. Just to postpone the inevitable, she brewed herself a hot cup of cappuccino and put on a Christmas carol that was all positive in her book:

> *Rocking around the Christmas tree*
> *At the Christmas party hop*
> *Mistletoe hung where you can see*
> *Every couple tries to stop*
> *Rockin' around the Christmas tree*
> *Let the Christmas spirit ring*
> *Later we'll have some pumpkin pie*
> *And we'll do some caroling*

Reluctantly, she brought her large plastic Christmas boxes from the upstairs storage closet and set them next to the tree. While the carols continued to play, she slowly started taking the ornaments down and carefully wrapping them in tissue for safekeeping.

Here was one that commemorated the birth of her daughter Leah. And there were a few other personalized ornaments that celebrated her son and youngest daughter. There were also several that had been given to her lovingly by her husband. One was a crystal heart; another was makeshift XOX that Brad had made by hand. These were ornaments that she wrapped with special care. They brought back a flood of fond family memories, and Lindsay vowed to keep better contact with her offspring.

Given the time difference, she first called her London-based daughter, Leah. "Honey, I was just looking at that baby-boots ornament and couldn't help but think about you," Momma said. "How are you? I hope you are having a great holiday season."

"Yes, it's great. But no snow," Leah responded. "Just that gray overcast sky that tends to last all winter long."

"Well, don't let it get you down," Mom advised. That was the atypical positive tone of the next fifteen minutes. In the process, she talked with the grandkids and her son-in-law. When her daughter got back on the phone, the younger woman was filled with compliments.

"Mom, you sound great. Are you having an unusually good Christmas?"

"Yes," Lindsay said without elaborating.

"That's just wonderful. Whatever sparkle dust is making that happen, I just hope it continues. Mom, you know I love you."

"I know that. Me too. Give everyone a big kiss and a hug for me," Lindsay answered and concluded the call. It was the happiest holiday call she had had in years, and it made her smile and feel all warm inside.

After a short while, she continued wrapping ornaments, destringing the lights, and packing them in storage boxes. It was sad looking at the naked Christmas tree. It had particularly added a bright, beautiful rainbow of colors this year. Given her gift-giving chores, she had certainly spent more time in its proximity than in past years.

The tree still smelled good, but she didn't want the hazard of a fire. She then took the trunk out of the stand and dragged the tree down the driveway to her mailbox.

She stood near the street and looked at the lingering but drying Christmas symbol. She sighed and trudged back into her warm home.

Probably best for safety's sake, she told herself. *But that doesn't mean Christmas is over. No way. Not this year.*

After cleaning up the dried needles on her floor, she watered her healthy poinsettia plants around the fireplace and was determined to retain the Christmas decorations atop the mantle. In the dining room, she decided to leave the bowlful of fragrant pinecones and the red and green candles that surrounded it—all this in a stubborn attempt to continue her newfound spirit of the holidays as long as possible.

There were two gift-giving occasions on her list for this particular day. She wrapped up a pair of gloves with a scarf and placed this note on the package.

Dear Mailman,

Thanks for all your help during the year. Hope you have a warm time during this Christmas season.

Next on the agenda: her gifts for the sanitation workers. In this case, she wrapped several packages of chocolates and attached the following note:

Dear guys,

Thanks for keeping this place so clean and being so dependable during the cold, snowy months. Hope you have a great Christmas season.

In each of the envelopes, she also included a crisp twenty-dollar bill since she figured that the civil servants could use a little cash to pay off their holiday bills.

She then walked all the packages down to the street, put the message for the postal worker inside her mailbox, and attached the sanitation workers' gifts to the dry Christmas tree.

She was grateful that she didn't have to wear a costume today. For a change, none of her gifts depended on being anonymous. That would change, she admitted to herself. She still had lots of gifts to give in the next few days and would need to disguise herself, if she wished to preserve her identity.

Meanwhile, she lit the Christmas candles on the dining room table and replayed more carols. Inspired by the music, she decided to touch base with her younger children.

She called her son first since he was in the same time zone as her in Atlanta.

"Todd, dear, this is your loving mother just saying hello. I was looking at the Christmas ornaments and saw that one with a baseball bat that commemorated your days in the Little League. You were quite a slugger in those days," she reminded him.

"Mom, wow, it's so nice to hear from you," Todd answered.

"Well, it's nice to hear your voice too," Mom answered. "What's up? Are the kids back in school?"

"Not till January 7. I think most school districts give two weeks off for travels and such." In this conversation, she learned that the family had visited the botanical gardens and seen several movies together. It was mostly small talk between Lindsay and her son. But unlike past years, it didn't feel forced or rushed. Both had a few laughs and nice recollections, and after about fifteen minutes, they both wished each other a great continuation of the holiday heart.

Finally, she called her youngest daughter, Carolyn, who lived in faraway Seattle.

"How is my baby girl?" Lindsay asked.

"Mom, I am so happy to hear from you. Hope you are having a fantastic holiday season. I was just thinking of you."

"As was I," Momma Brinkley said. "I was just holding that adorable Christmas ornament that you made for me in Girl Scouts and couldn't resist hearing your voice."

"The one of the goofy-looking Christmas tree?" her daughter asked.

"That's the one. Remember? It was a skinny, sick-looking little tree with stars all over?"

"I do remember. Everyone else was trying to make images of Santa Claus, but I couldn't draw that good."

"Well, it still looks skinny and sick, but it's beautiful," Mom reassured her.

They started talking about the holiday and some of the things that her young daughter and family had done in the past week. It included going to the mall, a chorale, and a few nice restaurants.

"Mom, you sound fantastic. Got a new boyfriend or something?" her precocious daughter teased her.

"No, not really. Not yet." Lindsay laughed. "But you never know. I am looking pretty hot these days."

After a few more laughs, she concluded the call with long-distance hugs and kisses.

That was a damn nice afternoon, Lindsay admitted to herself. Her conversations with her kids had never been so effortless. She smelled the pinecones and watched the candles flicker. She did look at the spot that housed the tree until this morning. Had it gone to its burial ground by now?

She peeked out the window to see if the sanitation workers had made the collection. Indeed, they had and presumably collected their Christmas gifts and envelopes. The tree was gone. But as she had discovered once again, the Christmas spirit lived on.

CHAPTER II

January 3

FEELING BUOYED BY yesterday's events and conversations with her kids, Lindsay looked at her list that cataloged her gift-giving intentions over the twelve days of Christmas. She recognized that she would need to restock her supply, if she hoped to complete her Good Samaritan mission.

She still had quite a few deliveries to make and tried to realign the list so that each day was manageable. She was also keenly aware that the more gifts she distributed, the more likely she would be discovered. For that reason, she had been more careful about her drop-off points, particularly to the growing number of video cameras that could identify her.

She thought there was little risk of that at the Ridge Hill Shopping Center. After all, as a shopper, her appearance would raise no suspicion. Besides, she wanted to touch base with Nick, the December Santa of the center, who had stopped by several days ago for a cup of cocoa. After her conversation with her younger daughter last night, she thought it might be fun to say hi to friendly man before embarking on her shopping spree.

To anticipate the moment, she put on the Eartha Kitt hit, "Santa Baby." Lindsay hadn't listened to the song for years and was somewhat surprised and tickled by the seductive nature of this Christmas classic:

> *Santa baby, just slip a sable under the tree for me*
> *I've been an awful good girl*
> *Santa baby, so hurry down the chimney tonight*
> *Santa baby, a '54 convertible too, light blue*
> *I'll wait up for you dear*
> *Santa baby, so hurry down the chimney tonight*
> *Think of all the fun I've missed*
> *Think of all the fellas that I haven't kissed...*

The more she listened to the sultry lyric, the more she looked forward to seeing Mr. Nick. She began to wonder if she was acting like a horny teenager. *Hardly*, she reasoned. Besides, it had been years since she actually took the time to share a cup of anything with an available man. Besides, she really did need to buy some gifts, and she would be in the neighborhood.

She called him in advance to see if he was available. He happily agreed and told her he would take his break at the coffee bar in the Cheesecake Factory. And so she donned her hat and sunglasses and headed for the sprawling shopping center.

On the way, she saw several ambulances heading in the opposite direction. *These are saints*, she told herself. *And I forgot to add them to my Christmas list.* Fortunately, as she knew, it wasn't too late. She could simply add more presents as long as she was in the retail neighborhood.

But first, she stopped at the restaurant and saw Nick at a table waiting for her. She walked slowly up to him and gave him a little peck on the cheek. "I've been thinking about you and just wanted to say hi again," she said.

"Well, I am glad you called, and I've been thinking about you." Nick twinkled his eyes at her. "I'm very proud of what you have been doing. It's impressive."

"Oh, come on. I'm an amateur at this." She blushed. "You've been doing it for years throughout the entire month of December."

He shrugged. "Yeah, but as Santa Claus, I'm supposed to do what I do. You? You're doing this with no desire for fame. It's so unselfish."

She took a sip of the cocoa he had preordered and placed on the table. She held up a finger and wanted to interject the thought that had been occurring to her over recent days. "That's the thing," she interrupted. "It's not so unselfish. Often, I feel like I get more out of it than the recipients. You think you're just helping the other people, but it actually helps me. I have never been happier during this season. Do you find that?"

Nick laughed. "Yep, that's the secret of good deeds."

"Don't misunderstand. I don't want to be discovered. That would ruin it," she added.

"Well, you've got to be super careful then. How many more days do you plan to risk exposure?"

"Four or five more days. By then, I think I'll be able to cross off most of the receivers of my Christmas gift giving."

Nick looked closely at her eyes and all the features of her face. He then took off his glasses and squinted. "Yep, that's what you look like slightly out of focus. I just saw another picture of you yesterday."

"Why?"

"It's innocent. The press stopped by to speak to me since they know I play Santa Claus. They thought I might know you. Don't worry, I told them I had never seen the woman in the pictures. Of course, nothing that they have is sharp focused. Still, they continue to search."

"Why?" she asked. "I'm not a criminal."

"No. The furthest thing from it." He chuckled. "It's just curiosity. And they want a scoop. They want to be the one that unmasks Santa's secret helper. So here's my advice to you. Vary your disguise. Get yourself another wig—maybe this one could be red. I love the fedora, but change up the hats. One day, a stocking cap. Another day, a cap. Change the coat every day. And the glasses."

"You're good at this," she complimented him.

"Just trying to protect your secret."

"You're good."

"We're both cut out of the same cloth," he added. "Besides, I want to take this beyond a cup of cocoa. We could be friends."

"We're already friends," she corrected him.

"We could be even better friends," he said. "When could we have that brunch?"

"I should have all my rounds completed by January 7. So how about January 8?"

He then rose to his feet, touched her hand, and gave her a kiss on the cheek. "Unfortunately, I have to get back to work now. But I will be seeing you on the eighth. I really look forward to it."

Lindsay followed him with her eyes and felt good about their budding relationship. However, she too had work to do this afternoon.

She started at TJ Maxx, where she found a nice-fitting auburn wig, new sunglasses, and a few different hats.

She then went to Dick's Sporting Goods and bought two dozen stress-relief squeeze balls. From there, she headed to the Container Store, which still featured Christmas ornaments. Luckily, she was able to find dozens of clear stars on sale. She then went to Walgreens, where she bought about forty Christmas candles. She dropped all the gifts in her trunk and finished up her shopping spree at Whole Foods, where she bought about one hundred red and green apples and bags to go with them.

Satisfied that she had supplies for the days ahead, she headed back to her home, which was only a few miles away.

First things first. She individually wrapped her stress balls (which, in a playful twist, were designed to look like beach balls). She then ran off twenty notes for her signature:

Dear ER nurse, doctor, or receptionist,

I was driving today and saw several ambulances. It made me appreciate the job you do each and every day and night. I hope this little gift can relieve some of the minute-by-minute stress of the job and remind you we all appreciate the job you do. Merry Christmas.

Santa's secret helper

She put them in a large bag for delivery.

First, she thought it would be great to try out her new costume. The auburn-red hair did look foreign on her, but she ended up thinking that yes, that's the idea.

She chose some wraparound sunglasses and topped off the outfit with a baseball cap—which was plain green. She had to smile because the entire effect was so definitely Christmassy.

She then drove to the nearest hospital and parked close to the emergency room entrance. Lindsay took a deep breath and dashed into the door to the admitting desk. Getting smarter about her drop-offs, she quickly glanced to see where the security camera was and turned her back to it. She then simply dropped off the bag with few words.

"This is for the staff of ER. Merry Christmas." Without waiting for a response—*poof!*—she was gone.

Feeling some pride that she had done something good for good people, she drove home with a sense of satisfaction. She imagined that those stress balls would be regularly used by the frazzled ER staff. Hey, it might even make them smile when they saw the beach-ball motif.

Once safely ensconced in her house, she played the remainder of "Santa Baby." She had to laugh at the brass of Eartha Kitt's Santa requests. Lindsay had asked less— just a little advice about the true goodwill sentiment and how to remain incognito. As usual, Santa had known just how to deliver. Yes, it was fun to have a kindred spirit. And yes, she wondered where it might lead.

CHAPTER 12

January 4

FOR SEVERAL YEARS, she had followed the horrific news stories about climate change. Various hurricanes had resulted in devastating catastrophes in New Orleans, Houston, Miami, Haiti, Dominica, New Jersey, and most recently, Puerto Rico.

The latest destruction happened as a result of Hurricane Maria. Weather forecasters had predicted it for the day, and it resulted in the near destruction of this American island. During the actual event, live footage was absolutely frightening. Often a newscaster would stand in the middle of the street, holding on to a light post for support, while waves would often crash to his left or his back. Some TV coverage showed buildings tumbling down, roofs and windows flying through the air, and cars completely under water.

Not surprisingly, dozens of people died, but it was also painful for the survivors. For weeks, 90 percent of the country had absolutely no power, no way to cry for help, no way to let relatives on the mainland know that they were still alive. About 70 percent of the survivors had no place to live, and 50 percent had no drinkable water.

As often happens, the National Guard came to the rescue. In this case, the governor of New York dispatched 125 National Guard soldiers to Puerto Rico to help remove debris and restore lines of communications.

In the aftermath of the hurricane, TV news footage of the disaster was heartbreaking. Fathers were walking down the streets waist-high in water. Mothers and babies were lined up outside the very few shelters to try to sleep in something other than a wet mattress. Many cried for help in Spanish. Some even carried signs of Gracias and hugged the National Guard soldiers as they debarked from the planes.

It was certainly a difficult way to spend the holiday for the citizens and the soldiers who would be separated from their own families in New York State. Just to wipe away the sad thoughts, she brought out lots of wrapping paper and the ornaments and began playing the José Feliciano hit "Feliz Navidad" to remind her that better times could be ahead.

Inspired by the beat of this Latino-American classic, she sang along and began wrapping 125 crystal star ornaments one by one. On each present, she attached the following note:

> Dear National Guard volunteer,
>
> I just wanted to add my gracias for helping the people of Puerto Rico. On behalf of all US citizens, you are a star. God bless you.
>
> X, Santa's secret helper.

She then looked in the Yellow Pages for National Guard recruiting stations and found a large one in the Bronx. She reasoned that it would provide the best chance for the gifts to be delivered.

She put all the presents in a big black Glad bag and taped a large sign to the outside. It read "Please deliver to the 125 National Guard heroes helping Puerto Rico."

Somewhat concerned about the reconnaissance capabilities of a military installation, Lindsay took special care to perfect her costume. She decided to apply extra makeup and super red lipstick. She figured a wide-brimmed hat would be a good change of pace and might help shield her from cameras. A large scarf and an oversize coat completed the ensemble.

Before she left, she looked on Google to make sure she had the right Spanish words for the delivery. Satisfied with her rehearsed pronunciation, she got in her car and drove to the recruiting station.

Once she arrived at the destination, she carried her bag into the recruiting office. Looking for surveillance cameras on the ceiling, she spied one and did her best to stay out of view. Then she quickly deposited her bag of gifts with one sentence: "Regales por los heroes." (Translation: gifts for the heroes.) She then waved gracias and quickly exited the building.

When she got to the car, she breathed a sigh of relief that she had most likely successfully delivered the presents without recognition. Still in character, she then whooped "Bueno, bueno" and drove home.

Later that night, she turned on the evening news and witnessed more of the devastation in Puerto Rico. People still lacked electricity and temporary housing. There was a short feature on jugs of water being delivered to the locals, many of whom had the arms outstretched for a fresh, uncontaminated sip.

Then the newscaster addressed the TV camera. "There is a bright spot in this human drama. Today, at about one p.m., a Good Samaritan delivered holiday thank-you presents to the Bronx National Guard people who are now in Puerto Rico. Evidently, she just dropped the bag of gifts and exited. Here is the man who accepted the package."

The newscaster walked over to the recruiter, whom Lindsay recognized.

"Who was she?" the newscaster asked.

"I have no idea," the recruiter answered. "She spoke Spanish and looked sort of Latino, so perhaps her origins were Puerto Rican. We have no good picture of her, but whoever she is, we just want to say thank you back on behalf of our National Guardsmen who are doing good deeds thousands of miles from home. And we will make sure they get your generous gifts."

By god, I'm getting better at this. Lindsay smiled and admitted.

The newscaster continued. In a close-up, he gave his most sincere entreaty: "If you know who this Good Samaritan is, give us a call. We'd like to meet her and get to know her a little better. And we are sure you would too."

"Enough, it's not your business!" Lindsay shouted to the TV screen. She then turned off the tube, lit the candles, and listened to more uplifting carols.

CHAPTER 13

January 5

SEVERAL WEEKS AGO, Al Krauter announced that Sprainbrook Nursery was going out of business. For sixty-eight years, this family-run horticultural center has been a source of plant life, lectures, and lawn products for thousands of families in Westchester County.

When Lindsay first heard the news, it made her so sad. This is where she bought the Christmas tree for decades. It's where she and her husband bought begonias and impatiens for the backyard gardens. It's where she found the best mums, Japanese maples, and arborvitae–all of which still thrive in the lawns of her home.

Beyond the products, the place had been a font of information and advice. Many of the employees had been there for decades and were familiar with most of the customers–many of whom they knew on a first-name basis.

In so many ways, it was a family. And losing the large greenhouse and grounds was like losing a family member.

Even with that disappointment, it was nothing compared to the sense of grief suffered by the owner, Mr. Al Krauter. As he wrote to many of his customers:

> With tears in my eyes and a very heavy heart, I am forced to make the gut-wrenching announcement that after sixty-eight years of service to the horticultural community. Sprainbrook Nursery, is closing its doors.
>
> The handwriting was on the wall for a long time, but I'm not a person to give in easily. I ended up pouring all my resources back into Sprainbrook Nursery. Sprainbrook has been my life, and I had hoped it would be able to take care of me until my death. That is not meant to be.
>
> I feel badly for my loyal customers. You have become my friends and inspiration. I will miss you, and I know you will miss Sprainbrook.
>
> Although this last month has been difficult on me, finding myself going through phases of mourning, depression, distress, disbelief, and the reality that the nursery will close, I have no personal regrets."

I would like to thank you for making my
life such a pleasant one.

Reading the e-mail, Lindsay couldn't help but sob.
Here was something far more than a business. It was a
labor of love for Al, his wife, his family, and his twenty-
five employees, many of whom had been with the nursery
for twenty-five to forty years.

Lindsay immediately knew she wanted to say thanks
for all their contributions. She also wanted to wish all the
employees good tidings for years ahead.

She had given some thought as to what to give this
group of hardworking gardeners who would now have
too much time on their hands. It was nuts to give them
gardening tools or beautiful plants. They had those in
abundance and would most likely not be using them in
the years ahead.

It was a personable group of people who would
undoubtedly want to keep contact with their many
friends. At the Papyrus paper and card shop, she found
dozens of beautiful greeting cards with lush plants on the
front–poinsettias, tulips, roses, birds of paradise, azaleas,
zinnias–everything from *A* to *Z*. The inside was blank,
so the sender could inscribe his or her own messages.
Perfect, Lindsay thought, although the mix of sadness and
joy still haunted her.

Just to capture the contraction, she searched her list
of songs to accompany her mixed moods. Her choice?
Simon and Garfunkel's "Silent Night / 7 O'clock News."

The song juxtaposes the sweetness of the holiday with the bad news of the day:

> *Silent night*
> *Holy night*
> *All is calm, all is bright*
> *Round yon virgin, mother and child*
> *(Newscast, overlapping with verse)*
> *This is the early evening edition of the news. The recent flight in the House of Representatives was over the open housing section*

Against this musical backdrop, Lindsay began to wrap twenty-five packets of cards. She privately wondered whom Al, his wife, and his workers might send them to. Friends? Distant relatives? Perhaps even some loyal customers who had become valuable contacts?

Once she had wrapped all the presents, Lindsay started on the note:

Dear Sprainbrookers,

I hope you know what an amazing difference you have made in so many people's lives. You have brought beauty, growth, and good nature to everyone around you for decades. We will miss you but want to thank you for all you've done, and we want to wish you Merry Christmases for many years to come. Keep in touch.

X, Santa's secret helper

She attached the message on each package and placed them all in a big black sack. On the front of the bag, she attached a piece of paper with the handwritten words "For the Sprainbrook owners and workers."

However, part of her did not wish to just sneak into the parking lot and never say goodbye. True, she could give her fond farewells and then leave the large bag of gifts–but that would be so easily traceable to her, and she had come to value her privacy as Santa's helper. So she devised a two-step process.

In part A, she would visit the nursery, buy a few plants as Lindsay Brinkley, and wish the Krauter family well with all their new endeavors. Even though the family had been going through these farewells for weeks, it was still emotional and full of hugs.

Two or three hours later, it was time for part B. In preparation, she costumed herself with the fedora, her shades, and a scarf. After parking, she deposited the bag in a wheelbarrow and brought it inside the large greenhouse but safely away from the busy cash registers.

With very mixed emotions, she slowly walked back to her car. Given the difference in time frames, she knew there was little chance anyone would ever be able to connect the dots and recognize her as the gift giver. She also instinctively knew there was little chance she would ever see the Krauter family again. As she admitted to herself, it's difficult when the supposedly happiest time of the year becomes the saddest.

CHAPTER 14

January 6

IN HER CRITIQUE of the season during past years, Lindsay often railed against the rampant commercialism of the holiday. "It's all sale, sale, sale, shop, shop, shop, buy, buy, buy," she would often say.

"Mom, don't be so negative," her kids would sometimes answer.

"You know, at its root, it's supposed to be a religious holiday. If I am not mistaken, a big Christian event happened around this time of year," she would tease her children.

Truth be told, Lindsay didn't have much room to talk in this regard. She had all her kids baptized and raised them in the Catholic religion, until they were about thirteen or fourteen when she figured they could make their own decisions. All of them emulated their mother and went to church only occasionally.

For the past seven or eight years, the woman had not been to church at all. When the scandals of priest abuse surfaced in the news, it gave her the excuse she wanted to talk about hypocrisy and sleep in on Sunday mornings. As in past years, she had not attended any of the advent Sundays or the always crowded Christmas ceremony. However, as the expression goes, once a Catholic . . . well, you know the rest.

Something about this particular season changed things for her. Like the great theological virtues laid out by Paul the Apostle, she had somehow rediscovered faith, hope, and charity. She had faith that her anonymous gifts might make a difference in the recipients' lives. She hoped that the presents would actually get to the right people, and from press and news reports, they had. And as for charity, well, Paul the Apostle thought it was the most important. Evidently, Lindsay Brinkley did too. She had freely given hundreds of thoughtful gifts to the people in her community this year, with no desire for fame or personal gratitude. In doing so, she had learned that giving is its own reward.

In view of all this, she felt a mightier magnetic link to the church than she had felt in years. In fact, she had planned to go to mass on the Feast of the Epiphany for the past week or so. Why on that particular day? Well, for one thing, it gibed with her new charitable preoccupation. Also called the Feast of the Three Kings, this big feast commemorates the three wise men that followed the brightest star in the sky in hopes of bringing gifts to baby Jesus. One brings gold. One brings frankincense. One brings a thing called myrrh, which is like a balm.

Lindsay planned to bring something else to this January 6 mass. She had bought beautiful white candles for the choir members. She figured it would be about twelve singers, so she had purchased twenty-four long tapers, coupled them, and tied a bright-red ribbon around each bundle. Lindsay attached the following note, which was taped to each bundle:

> Dear choir member,
>
> When you raise your beautiful voice, you remind us all of the true meaning of Christmas. Hope it has been wonderful for you and your family. Merry, merry.
>
> X, Santa's secret helper

Yes, but how would she be able to deliver them without being identified? Once again, she figured two trips were in order. Wearing her red wig, stocking cap, dark shades, and heavy coat, she entered St. Andrew's Church a full hour before mass would begin.

There was no one else there, just the sacred quiet and beautiful shafts of light from the stained glass windows. Surreptitiously, she deposited each bundle on each chair of the choir box. Her estimate of the choir singers was about right. There were actually eleven chairs, so she put the extra bundle in her coat and exited the church.

She was surprised how good it felt to be inside the church again. Perhaps it was the mystery of the environment. Perhaps it was majesty of all those red drapes on the altar. More likely, it was the timing. For the past several weeks, she had been doing a very Christian thing, and it just felt good to be there.

When she returned back to her home, she folded her costume and donned her own clothes. No need to mask who she was. Besides, some neighbors would undoubtedly know her. Since there was little risk of exposure, there was no need to continue the charade during the mass. Besides, it would be fun to see some familiar folks in the parish.

She arrived about a minute before the service started. The place was packed, but she could clearly see the choir. Some of the members were proudly showing their candles to their friends in the pews. Many were proudly smiling.

When the priest entered, the choir began to sing the carol most often associated with the Epiphany:

We three kings of Orient are
Bearing gifts, we traverse afar
Field and fountain, moor and mountain
Following yonder star
O Star of wonder, star of night
Star with royal beauty bright
Westward leading, still proceeding
Guide us to thy perfect light

At the culmination of the carol, Lindsay almost applauded but soon realized that that's not what one does in church. No, the parishioners simply nod appreciation to one another, and the choir nods back. Even so, Lindsay privately felt like a benevolent spark plug that might have given the singers a little extra juice.

Within twenty-five minutes, the pastor took the pulpit and welcomed the congregation. He stressed the value of charity and even referenced the mystery woman who had been giving presents to strangers this season. He continued, "Perhaps you have read about her. Well, we should all have that spirit."

Lindsay was afraid to look to the right or left. Was the priest talking about her? Were people looking at her? Most likely not. Just to make sure, she just stared straight ahead.

Following his cheerful sermon, the priest gave communion to those who wished it, the choir sang an exit carol, and the crowd streamed out of the church smiling and nodding to one another.

At the door, the priest recognized Lindsay. "Mrs. Brinkley, it's so nice to see you again," he said in his friendliest voice, without any sense of guilt or accusation.

"Well, it's nice be here again," she answered with a smile.

Soon, she saw many of her neighbors, who also gave her a warm hug and a welcome. Several invited her for coffee at the nearby diner, but Lindsay demurred. She already had plenty of lovely warmth for one day.

CHAPTER 15

January 7

LINDSAY HAD ONE more goodwill mission to accomplish on her Christmas list, and it would arguably be the most difficult to execute. It would entail the delivery of about one hundred packages to people in the community who might actually recognize her.

Yesterday, at church, Father McMahon admitted that January 6 technically and liturgically ends the Christmas season, but he hoped everyone would keep the spirit of charity alive. For a brief moment, Lindsay thought that could give her an out from attempting this last act of kindness. *Nah*, she told herself. *I've come so far. I may as well complete the whole shebang.*

Her target for this delivery? The one hundred teachers in the village.

Ever since her kids had been in the Dobbs school district, she had admired the selfless dedication that these heroes exhibit. Inevitably, they suffer criticism from disgruntled parents. They have to spend late nights planning lessons and correcting papers. They are expected to participate in extracurriculars like the football games, the science club, and junior achievement. They have to deal with school boards that constantly are changing the goalposts and insist that their district must be better than the one in the next village.

It must be exhausting. And yet given her own family experience, she truly believed that the teachers have the biggest influence on a kid's self-esteem and future plans other than the student's own parents.

How to let them know they are truly appreciated? How to recognize them?

How to applaud them?

True, all the teachers just had a long Christmas vacation, but that would come to a screeching halt today, and there would be little rest until the dog days of summer.

To prepare for the big delivery day, Lindsay completed some of her shopping last night and rose before 6:00 a.m. She already had more than two hundred red and green apples in her storage area but knew that she would need about four hundred more to make a meaningful impact. Consequently, she stocked up at the local A&P, the Grand Union, and Stew Leonard's supermarkets. She also had her stash of more than one hundred small paper bags with handles from Walgreens.

To put herself in the mood for giving, she listened to Annie Lennox and Al Green sing "Put a Little Love in Your Heart."

Think of your fellow man
Lend him a helping hand
Put a little love in your heart
You see it's getting late
Oh, please don't hesitate
Put a little love in your heart
And the world will be a better place
For you and me

Almost to the beat, she put six red and six green apples in each of the paper bags. On the front, she attached the following note:

Dear teachers,

Thanks for making our world a better place, especially for all our children. Please know that you embody the holiday spirit and make a big difference every single day. Merry, merry. Welcome back.

X, Santa's secret helper

And now came the hard part: how to get these packages to the teachers without linking them directly to her? She had envisioned various disguises but feared that the masquerade wouldn't hold after repeated deliveries to the grade school, the middle school, and the high school. Besides, each delivery would take too long. Inevitably, she believed townspeople would recognize her despite her best camouflage.

No, so instead of dropping off the apples undercover, she decided to accomplish this mission without ever setting foot on the school entrances.

Instead, she hired three different limo companies and invited them to bring their cars to the large parking lot at the Cross County Shopping Center in Yonkers. She instructed them to be there at 7:00 a.m. to help load some bags into their trunks.

There were three other stipulations:

1. She would pay cash.
2. They had to make their individual deliveries by 8:00 a.m.
3. They should not be afraid of her look. As Lindsay explained to them, "I have accidentally, but severely, burned my face. It is wrapped up like a mummy. That's why I want you to make the delivery. I don't want to scare any of the kids."

All three limo companies eagerly agreed, especially since the woman said she would pay in cash.

Once in the lot, she truly did wrap her face with a rolling bandage just like a mummy. Then she wore her sunglasses. There was no chance anyone could ever recognize her.

At 7:00 a.m., the first limo arrived. He loaded twenty-five bags. She gave him an envelope with the agreed-upon money and the address of the village grade school.

At 7:03 a.m., the next limo arrived. He loaded thirty bags for the middle school.

At 7:06 a.m., the last limo came and drove the remaining forty-five bags to the high school.

As Lindsay watched the last black car leave the lot, she climbed into her Jeep Cherokee, unwrapped her bandages, and proudly drove home. On her way past the high school, she did steal a look at the limo man carrying the apple bags into the school. She also couldn't help but notice that there was a news truck right behind him. A man in a suit was obviously making a newscast, since there was a man with a video camera just behind him.

Rather than linger, Lindsay just chuckled and said, "Good luck, guys. You will never meet Santa's secret helper." After a few minutes, she was able to pull into her driveway, satisfied that her private charitable act would remain private.

Later that day, she did call Nick to tell him that she pulled off her most complicated mission without discovery. He congratulated her and reaffirmed that he would be there tomorrow for that long-awaited brunch date.

Later that night, she did turn into the local news and hear about her escapade.

According the newscaster, "Christmas apples were delivered to all the teachers in Dobbs Ferry this morning on their first day back from the holiday, courtesy of Santa's secret helper. But she didn't deliver them. According to the limo driver, she did orchestrate the whole thing but had been severely burned, and her face was covered with bandages. We checked all the local hospitals, but there were no such recent emergencies."

The newsman shook his head in exasperation. "Who is she? We're going to try to find out today. We're going to track all her deliveries and try to see any relevant photos, because we think you'd like to know. Stay with us. Hopefully, we'll find her, because we'd all like to meet her."

As Lindsay sipped a ginger ale, she quietly uttered, "It's not going to happen, man." She then smiled, quite satisfied that her twelve days of gift giving had been accomplished quite privately, cleverly, and secretly.

CHAPTER 16

January 8

NICK ARRIVED AT her house around 11:00 a.m., in anticipation of their noon brunch. As soon as he walked through the door, he gave her a big hug and kiss and told her how very happy he was to see her again. He also communicated how privately proud he was of all she had done during the holiday season.

"I think I got my whole list done without ever being found out by anyone other than you." She beamed.

"I was just lucky at Ridge Hill to view your license plate. The cameras actually caught you walking to your car. It's amazing how advanced security has become in these days."

"And how careful one has to be to avoid the glare," she added with a laugh. She then poured each of them a cup of coffee and invited him to make himself comfortable in the living room.

She had lit the fireplace in advance and then hit the button on her stereo for her favorite Christmas song. It was the Nat King Cole standard:

Chestnuts roasting on an open flame
Jack Frost nipping at your nose
Yuletide carols being sung by a choir
And folks dressed up like Eskimos
Everybody knows a turkey and some mistletoe
Help to make the season bright
Although it's been said many times, many ways
Merry Christmas to you

"It's my favorite too." Nick smiled. "I often listen to that song when I am in character."

"As far as I can tell, it's a permanent part of your character to be nice." She smiled back. "Your advice on the costumes really helped. It gave me even more confidence to make the big actions possible."

Just then, the doorbell rang, and Lindsay excused herself to open the door. On the porch was a newsman with a microphone. A cameraman was behind him.

"Mrs. Lindsay Brinkley," the newsman asked. "My name is Carl Johnson with WABC."

"Yes, how can I help you?" she answered tentatively.

"On behalf of all our viewers, we are trying to track down Santa's secret helper, and we have a hunch it could be you."

"That's impossible," she protested. "I've heard of her too, but it's definitely not me."

"Well, we have several pictures from several of the deliveries, and some seem to match."

Overhearing the conversation, Nick joined her in the doorway. "Let me see those pictures," he demanded. As he scrolled through several surveillance snapshots, he shook his head. "That's ridiculous. The woman in this picture has red hair. Here's one with a woman in a man's hat. They don't even look like her."

"Maybe they were disguises," the newsman suggested.

"No, my dear wife here spends her days making me chicken noodle soup and keeping the house tidy. I work from home and know that she is here all the time. Right, dear?" He then put his arm around Lindsay.

"Right honey, but I may make you chicken barley soup today," she good-naturedly corrected him.

"I'd really prefer chicken noodle," Nick mock protested.

"OK, chicken noodle it is," she lovingly answered.

The newsman had become exasperated. "Enough about the chicken soup, you two. Are you Santa's secret helper or not?"

"I am not," she answered firmly.

"And I should know, she is not," Nick added with stern emphasis. "Now if you gentlemen will not get off our private property, my wife and I will be forced to call the police." He then brought out his cell phone and started punching some numbers.

"No, put that away," the newsman interrupted the dialing. "It's probably our mistake. Sorry to have intruded. Have a great afternoon." He then gestured to his cameraman to kill the tape and addressed him. "Mike, let's go to the next address on our list." He pulled out his notebook and headed to the van.

Exhibiting sweetness and light, the couple stood arm in arm in the doorway and waved goodbye. Before they would break character, they kept their eye on the news van until it exited the driveway and drove down the street.

As soon as it was out of viewing frame, Lindsay closed the door and laughed uproariously. She then put her arms around Nick and gave him a big kiss on the lips.

"Wow, you are good." She giggled.

"I've had a lot of experience playing a role–although this one was a little different from the one I am used to playing."

"Well, it seemed to come natural to you." As the words came out of her mouth, Lindsay did feel that being next to him felt natural to her. It had been a long time since she had been in someone's arms. *Who exactly knows where this might lead?* She reminded herself to not get ahead of her skis. However, it did feel good to be with such a kindred spirit who could complete her sentences and instinctively be on her wavelength. *Perhaps this is my Christmas present*, she thought.

Quietly, she gave him a tighter hug and another kiss.

"Do you have an appetite for that chicken noodle soup," she teased with a twinkle in her eye.

"I hate chicken noodle soup." He chuckled. "And chicken barley."

"Good, I made a reservation at Maud's Restaurant."

"Let's go. I'm with you," Nick said.

She took his hand, walked to the car, and felt like a Christmas kid after all these years.

EPILOGUE

THE NEXT MORNING, her daughter Leah called her mom and invited the woman to come to London for Valentine's Day. "Valentine's Day?" Lindsay chortled. "I'm still celebrating Christmas."

"Are you OK, Mom?"

"I've never been better," Lindsay answered, and she promised she would think about a trip to Great Britain in February.

Within the next few days, the media stopped chasing Santa's secret helper, perhaps because all the gifts had been delivered, perhaps because the shelf life of that story had a natural expiration date of January 10.

Lindsay adopted a rescue dog from the Yonkers Animal Shelter. It was a Labrador-poodle mix. She named him Kris Kringle. It's a nod to her favorite time of year and her new best friend, Nick Carter. Incidentally, they plan to visit Jamaica next year, right after December 25–that is, unless dozens of new worthy causes merit more loving-care packages in the ensuing weeks.

CPSIA information can be obtained
a. www.ICGtesting.com
Printed in the USA
EVHW03*1039200318
511074BV00005B/25/P